5|22

To all the children who believe that friendship and kindness make a happier world.

First published in Great Britain 2022 by Farshore
An imprint of HarperCollins*Publishers*
1 London Bridge Street, London SE1 9GF

farshore.co.uk

HarperCollins*Publishers*
1st Floor, Watermarque Building, Ringsend Road
Dublin 4, Ireland

Text copyright © Farshore 2022
Interior illustration copyright © Dynamo 2022
The moral rights of the author and illustrator have been asserted.

Special thanks to Rachel Delahaye.
With thanks to Speckled Pen for their help in the development of this series.

ISBN 978 0 00 851245 3
Printed and bound in the UK using 100% renewable electricity at CPI Group (UK) Ltd

1

SUPER CUTE

THE KINDNESS CAROUSEL

PIP BIRD

Farshore

ZIM-ZOOMERS

SUNFLOWER NURSERY

GHOST TRAIN

PARASOL POND

CUSHION MOUNTAIN

THE KINDNESS CAROUSEL

TWIRLING TEACUPS

CONTENTS

CHAPTER ONE

Just in the Middle of a Dream

Inside a little house that swung from a branch of the liquorice tree, Cami the cloud was dreaming a glorious dream . . . She was having a picnic in the dipsy daisy meadows as the popsicle parrots circled above, filling the sky with rainbow colours. Her very best

1

friends were there, which made it the best kind of dream, and she was about to take a bite of a dreamy sugar puff peach, when – TINKLE TINKLE TINKLE – a noise woke her up.

Cami was absolutely certain that the delicate chime was the sound of sweetie pies as they put-putted across the morning sky. And what was that rustling and bustling? It must be the World of Cute waking up!

Cami stretched out her cloud fluff. Then it dawned on her. She sprang out of her snooze basket and bumped her fluffy head on the ceiling.

'Oh my goodness, today is the fair!' she cried. 'THE SUNFLOWER FAIR!'

She flew quickly out of her house.

But instead of daylight, she found herself floating in the deep, dark blue sky that belonged to night. The tinkling she had heard was not the giggle of early morning sweetie pies, but the sound of the stars playing twinkle-chase. The rustle and bustle was not the World of Cute waking up, but the snuffles of allsort bugs, fast asleep in the nooks of the liquorice tree.

'Oh! I'm awake far too early,' Cami said sadly.

She floated back into her little home, sank into her soft basket and tried to get back to sleep. But it was impossible. Every time she closed her eyes, her imagination danced with colours and sounds and oodles of excitement. The Sunflower Fair was just hours away!

Cami had never been to the Sunflower Fair before, but her friend Sammy the sloth had told her all about it. It celebrated the start of summer, and it was all about happiness and sunshine. There were fairground rides and games, fun competitions and treats of every flavour imaginable. Everyone wore something that made them feel summery.

Best of all, Cami loved the sound of the glow cakes. They were made only once a year by the Sunshine Cakery: a secret bakery hidden deep in the buttercup fields, run by talented sugar mice and honey combs.

Cami smiled woozily as she remembered Sammy's description of the delicacy. *'The icing is so bright it makes you leap for joy; the topping is so fizzy it makes your tongue tingle; the middle is so yummy it makes your tummy gurgle . . .'*

Cami imagined leaping, giggling and gurgling with her friends as they munched the delicious treats under the new summer sun.

'I'm going to be the only cloud in the sky!' Cami said to herself in delight. 'But I'll be white and puffy and filled with nothing but happiness. It's going to be the most perfect day ever. And best of all, I'm sharing it with the super cutes!'

She snuggled down in her cloud basket, closed her eyes and thought back to the time she'd first met her special friends on the way to the Cuteness Competition in Charm Glade. Although everyone had started off nervous and shy, by the end of the day they were jumping with joy and happy to have made some new friends. It was the start of something truly special. Their next get-together had been Sammy's magical, mystical sleepover party, and then came the Friendship Festival, and the Adventure Weekend at Cute Camp . . . Whenever the super cutes were together, they always managed to have the best time.

By the time Cami had finished thinking all these happy thoughts, her brain was buzzing so much that there was absolutely no chance of going back to sleep.

'It's no good,' she said to herself. 'I'm just too excited!'

'Shhh,' hissed Albi, an allsort bug whose snooze hole was just outside her door. 'We're trying to sleep.'

'Sorry, Albi!' said Cami, her cloud fluff blushing. 'I'm so sorry.'

'If you stop saying sorry, I might be able to get back to sleep.'

'Sorry . . .' said Cami. 'Oh dear, I think I'd better do something to keep me busy, or my excitement's going to wake the whole town.'

'Good idea,' grumbled Albi.

'I know! I'll make my Summer Gift,' Cami said to herself, very, very quietly.

Sammy had said that all the cutes contributed a gift to the Sunny Lucky Dip, so that everyone went home with a little memento of the day. It could be anything, from homemade treats to a special poem to a crafty craft.

'What shall I make?' Cami pondered. 'What's a symbol of sunshine and summer joy?'

Her mind drifted back to her dream, picnicking beneath the bright popsicle parrots.

Aha! She knew the perfect thing. Something that symbolised the changing of the seasons with spring showers meeting summer sunshine: a rainbow suncatcher!

She concentrated her happy thoughts to make multicoloured rain. Then she mixed her rain with glue and poured it into a rainbow-shaped mould and hung it from a ceiling hook to dry out. Just as she finished, a beam of sunlight burst through the windowpane, lighting up the rainbow suncatcher and spraying light all round her room. It flickered like a fabulous disco!

'It's perfect!' Cami gasped, twirling in the multicoloured light. 'And best of all, it's morning!'

She popped her head out of the door of her little house and looked up. Yes, there were the flocks of sweetie pies, lemony-yellow custard tartlets with meringue wings. They left icing sugar trails as they spun on the air currents. Above them, a big blue sky stretched from Vanilla Valley to Marshmallow Canyon to the Sandy Beaches and beyond.

'Perfect. Absolutely perfect!' Cami squealed.

She flew out and up into the air. The sun warmed the dew on her cloud fluff, making her steam like a dumpling and sparkle like a gummy glitter chew.

'Yippeeeee!' she cried, loop-the-looping over and over again. 'It's here! It's here!'

'What's here?' grumbled Albi the allsort bug, emerging from his dark hole to see what the fuss was about.

'The Sunflower Fair!'

'What's so special about this Sunflower

Fair?' Albi snorted.

'Absolutely everything!' Cami cried. 'I've never been before, but I heard it's one of the best days ever on the cute calendar. You should come, too.'

'And leave my cool, dark liquorice hole?' said Albi with a sniff. 'No, thank you very much.'

'Oh, please come, Albi. You might be surprised. Look, even the sun's excited!' Cami said, pointing to the blazing

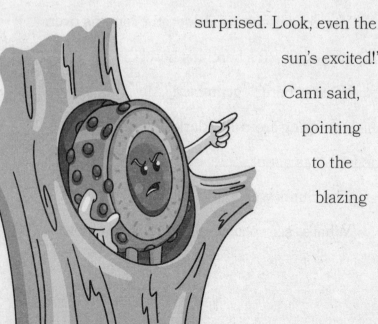

ball in the sky. 'He's
wearing a new visor
for the occasion.'

'I heard it's a hot
fashion item,' the sun said
with a wink.

'Well, I think you look very *cool*!' Cami
giggled.

'Huh,' said Albi, disappearing into his hole
again. Cami felt a bit sad that he wasn't coming
to the fair.

'Speaking of fashion . . . everyone always
wears something sunny to the fair.' The sun
wrapped one of his rays around Cami. It
shimmered and shone like a sash of golden silk.

'Thank you so much!' Cami gasped. 'This is amazing!'

Cami rushed inside, popped her suncatcher in a little soft pouch and set off for the Wishing Tree to meet her friends. Her sunray sash fluttered out behind her like the tail on a cloud-shaped kite. And Cami just knew this day was going to be *perfect*.

CHAPTER TWO

Bursting with Happiness

Some of the super cutes were already at the Wishing Tree. As Cami got closer, she felt her fluff rumble with anticipation. There was Sammy the sloth wearing gold-rimmed spectacles, Micky the mini-pig in a little yellow tie and Louis the labradoodle, who had

splattered himself in yellow paint! Everyone had worn something to represent the sunshine. It was perfect. Absolutely perfect!

'Yoo-hoo!'

Cami looked down to see a cartwheeling pineapple. Pip was glistening with gold glitter from her toes to her spiky top. Beside her was Dee the dumpling kitty, who had knitted herself a yellow cardigan.

Cami stopped above the Wishing Tree and looked down at her very best friends all gathered together.

'You all look SO summer-tastic!' Cami said.

But nobody heard her, because her soft voice was drowned out by the thunder of hooves.

Lucky the lunacorn was galloping towards them in a billowing cloud of sherbet. When she got closer, they could see that it wasn't sherbet at all! She had covered her horn in honey butter, which had attracted a flock of bright yellow butterlick bow-ties. Their ribbon wings fluttered happily.

'That's brilliant, Lucky!' Pip squealed, doing a backflip and landing on her head.

'Looks like you forgot to put glitter on your bottom, Pip!' Dee said, pointing at Pip's upturned end. The kitty cat quickly pulled some sparkles from her craft pockets and threw them on the pineapple's underside. 'There you go, glitterbum!'

Pip giggled uncontrollably. Soon *everyone* was laughing. There was such excitement in the air.

'Let's go!' Louis barked.

'We can't go,' said Lucky, doing a head count. 'Someone is missing.'

'We're not going anywhere until all the super cutes are here,' Dee agreed.

'Cami's not here,' said Sammy, scratching his bottom with concern.

'I'm here, I'm here!' Cami cried from overhead.

But Louis was barking again, drowning out Cami's voice. 'I'm itching my inks to paint some sunflowers!' he said, and he twitched his magical nose, which could turn into any pen, crayon or paintbrush, and accidently splattered the Wishing Tree. 'Oops.'

'Careful, Louis,' Sammy said. 'The Wishing Tree is very sensitive. Now, where is that lovely little cloud?'

'I'm here, I'm here!' Cami repeated – but now the Wishing Tree was making a huge WHOOSH as it rustled its branches and shook off the yellow paint, and Cami's voice was lost all over again.

Rain on a summer's day, Cami thought. That will get their attention!

Fun rain was Cami's special trick. She often poured down miniature items to the delight of her friends. They never knew what was coming – it was always a surprise.

Cami thought hard about what would be

best for this occasion. She made her cloud tummy rumble and then – *Pop!* – out came a fun rain, fitting for a summer fair.

The super cutes clapped with delight at the sunflowers, which fell around them giggling and squealing before popping into thin air.

Then they looked up.

'Cami!' Micky said, delighted. 'There you are!'

'What a brilliant way to start the day,' Lucky said. 'A sunflower shower! Thanks, Cami.'

Cami blushed with happiness.

'What's that you're wearing?' Micky said, peering at her sash. 'It looks like a ribbon but it's see-through.'

Louis leaped up and stroked the ribbon, but his paw went right through it. 'It's not there!' he said in amazement.

'How wonderful. A vanishing ribbon,' Dee said. 'I wish I had some of that in my craft pockets.'

'It's actually a ray of sunshine,' Cami said. 'The sun gave it to me this morning.'

'**WOW**,' the super cutes gasped.

'This is a very good sign,' said Sammy. 'If the sun is giving out his sunrays, it means good times are ahead.'

'I'm already having a good time,' Cami said, looking round at the faces of her beautiful friends. 'The super cutes are back together.'

'Hooray for the super cutes!' the friends all cheered.

Sammy coughed for attention. 'For the past three hundred and fifty four years, the Sunflower Fair has always taken place at the Petal Pasture, which is the other side of Charm

Glade,' he said. 'We'd better get a move on or we'll miss the opening parade.'

'We can't be late,' Micky said, bringing out his pocket watch. 'I don't like being late. Not at all. Besides, I don't want to miss a minute of fun!'

'All right, let's go! Anyone who wants a ride, hop on!' said Lucky. 'Just don't squash the butterlick bow-ties.'

Sammy, Pip and Dee sat on Lucky's back. Louis ran alongside with Micky, who did piggy-rolls to keep up. Cami floated above them all, happy as a cloud. And they began to sing . . .

We're all off to the Sunflower Fair
Wearing something yellow.

We'll be laughing all day long,

Everybody join in our Sunflower Song.

Say it loud and sing it strong!

YELL-O! YELL-O! YELL-O!

Above them, the sweetie pies whistled the tune and the topply tulips that grew along the roadside wiggled on their stems. The sun beamed overhead and Cami waved. But when she looked down again, she noticed that Pip was looking a bit distressed.

'Are you okay, Pip?' she asked.

'Oh, you know,' said the little pineapple. 'It's just that I'm worried about a whole day in the sunshine. I'll get over-ripe and squishy.'

26

'You're a tropi-cool fruit, I understand, Pip,' said Cami, who knew how easily this exotic pineapple overheated. 'I promise I'll stay near.' She sat above Pip's head to cast some shade and they went on their way.

'What shall we do when we get there, Sammy?' Louis said. 'Sammy?'

Dee nudged the snoozing sloth, who woke with a start. 'There's a million

honey bees in the bee castle at Bumble Farm,' he said, quite randomly. His eyelids blinked like the wings on a butterlick bow-tie. Then he shook out his camouflaging fur, which had turned as white as Lucky's wing feathers, and repositioned his wonky glasses. 'Did someone ask me a question?' he said.

'We were asking about what to see at the fair,' Dee giggled.

'We'll be spoilt for choice,' Sammy said. 'But there are two things we must absolutely do. One – we must eat glow cakes.'

'Yummy!' declared Pip, leaping for joy and spiking Cami with her prickly leaves. 'Sorry!'

'What's the other?' said Micky, getting out a

little notepad and pen.

'And the other is to go on a ride,' said Sammy. 'Last year, the most popular ride was the D-Force.'

'D as in Dee?' said Dee.

'D as in dogs-like-to-go-fast,' said Louis.

'D as in double fun!' said Lucky.

'D as in definitely!' said Pip. 'I love going fast. The faster, the better.'

Cami felt herself turn grey. She gulped and dropped a raindrop on Pip's head.

Pip looked up. 'What's up, Cami?'

'D as in disaster!' wailed Cami. 'I've never been good with rides. Not since I got caught in Cyclone Chaos during the Winter Storms and was blown at a hundred miles an hour out to sea.'

'Oh yes,' said Sammy. 'Worst storm in recent history, caused by warm air from the atmosphere coming into contact with the streams of stone-cold cuteness and creating a –'

'Nothing's scary when you're with us, Cami,' Lucky interrupted. Sammy could talk about facts all day! 'We'll take good care of you. You might even enjoy it.'

'Pssst!' A noise came from the side of the road. It was the dipsy daisies, who were throwing dandelion seeds in the air.

Micky stooped down. 'Did you say something?' he asked the little flowers.

The dipsy daisies whispered in Micky's

ear. Micky looked up at the others and repeated what they said. 'The dipsy daisies heard from Tom Tom the sushi mouse, who heard from the funny bunnies, who saw the fair being set up, that there's a new fairground ride this year and it's super scary.'

Whoa! The super cutes all looked at each other with their mouths open.

'Well, I never!' said Sammy. 'I didn't know that.'

'There'll be big queues of cutes lined up to try it, I bet!' Pip said with excitement.

Cami shrank a little and felt her tummy rumble with fright. She was so used to floating in plenty of space, drifting slowly on the sky breezes, that just the thought of scary rides and crowds of cutes was a bit too much!

'Are you okay, Cami?' Pip asked. 'You just got smaller.'

Cami looked down at her brilliant friend, backflipping in excitement beneath her. She took a deep breath. 'Absolutely!' she said, pulling herself together and puffing out her chest. 'It's going to be an amazing day!'

CHAPTER THREE

Trouble in a Maze

At the entrance to the Petal Pasture, the super cutes were greeted by two enormous flowers. It was hard to tell if they were swaying in the wind or dancing to the boppy fair music that drifted over to them on the wind.

'Welcome!' said one.

'Come well!' said another.

'We're here for the fair,' said Louis, leaping to see over their heads to the field beyond.

'Of course,' said the first flower. 'It's the other side of the Holler Hedge Maze. Enter.'

'Enter and be amazed,' said the other.

The flowers smiled and stepped aside to let them through.

'This is so exciting,' Cami gasped, hovering closely over Pip.

'And it's not just an attraction,' Sammy said. 'The maze is designed so that there's not a rush of cutes through the main gates all at the same time!'

'I'm terrible at mazes,' Pip whined. 'They make my head hurt.'

'And I want to get there as soon as possible,' said Dee. 'What if we get lost and miss all the entertainment?'

'Leave this to me, my fellow super cutes,' Sammy said, twitching his nose. 'I've been studying this maze since I was a slothling. And if we get into too much trouble, the hedges will holler for help and someone will come and find us.'

Sammy marched through the gates and into the high-walled maze, with the others following. But after five minutes of twists and turns, he stopped and scratched his head.

'Fleas, Sammy?' said Pip.

'No, I thought there was a right turn here,' he said, itching his bottom. 'And over there, I'm sure there's meant to be a clearing with a bench.' He frowned and scratched his head *and* his bottom, as if the combination might help. 'Oh dear! If everything I thought I knew about this maze is wrong, then I don't know where we're going and we're going to get very lost indeed. I must be losing my sloth marbles.' Sammy shook his head and sighed.

'I don't think so, Sammy,' said Cami kindly. 'You're the smartest cute I know. Perhaps you just studied the maze upside down?'

'Maybe I did,' Sammy muttered, scratching and blinking and turning in circles. 'Yes, that must be it. Thank you, Cami.'

'Shall we ask the hedge to holler?' Lucky said.

'No, no, I'm sure we can manage!' Sammy said, turning in circles three more times.

Micky took out a notepad. 'Perhaps I should keep track of where we're going,' he said.

'There's an easier way than that,' Lucky said with a grin. 'Some of us can fly. We can guide everyone through the maze!

Isn't that right, Cami?'

Cami looked down at her pineapple friend. It really was very hot and sunny. 'I'm not sure if I can leave Pip,' she said anxiously.

'I'll be fine,' Pip said. 'Sweaty and smooshy, but fine. Let's get to the fair!'

Lucky and Cami took to the sky. Up here, Cami could see the route right through the maze to the other side. And she also saw the funfair, glittering in the distance.

'It looks SO exciting,' Lucky gasped.

'Yes, and so . . . busy!' Cami replied.

From up high, she could see some of the rides the Sunflower Fair was famous for, such as the Twirling Teacups and the Popcorn Explosion,

where little popcorn-shaped carriages shot high into the air. A few worried raindrops popped up on her forehead.

It's going to be fun, she told herself, wiping them away. Trying new things will be fun, fun, fun.

'Okay everyone, follow us!' Lucky cried.

'Left, left, right, right, left, right, left. That's it!'

Skipping with excitement as the candy floss smells and funfair bells got closer and closer, the super cutes made their way through the maze. The hedges didn't holler, but instead rustled and whispered encouragement as they passed: *'You can do it. Go super cutes!'*

'I can see the exit,' Cami called. 'We're nearly there.'

'Wait.' Dee held up her paw and everyone stopped. 'Where's Sammy?'

'I haven't seen him for at least ten minutes,' Micky said, sounding worried. 'Can you spot Sammy from up there, you two?'

Cami and Lucky looked, but Sammy was nowhere to be seen. He had completely vanished.

'Oh no!' Pip sobbed. 'Poor Sammy, lost and all alone in the maze!'

'TOOT, TOOT! Out the way!'

The super cutes gasped as a huge hot air balloon in the shape of banana drifted towards them. Inside were two people they knew very well.

'Nana Banana!' said Pip with a flip, landing with a thump on her glitterbum.

'And Sammy!' Louis barked. 'Sammy, what are you doing all the way up there?'

Sammy grinned down at them. 'I fell asleep and the hedges hollered and Nana Banana came to the rescue,' he explained.

Cami spotted the patches of green on Sammy's fur. 'Oh, Sammy! You must have fallen asleep in a hedge and camouflaged yourself.'

Nana Banana chuckled and patted Sammy on the head. 'I spotted his golden glasses, flashing in the sunlight,' she said. 'He was quite dazed when I woke him up and he didn't know where he was, so he came aboard. Why don't

you all come aboard too? We can fly the rest of the way!'

'Hooray!' cheered the super cutes.

Nana lowered a walking plank and the cutes clambered up into the basket that dangled below the balloon. With a blast of warm, banana-scented air, the airship climbed back into the sky.

'Popsicle parrots!' Cami shouted. 'Look, everyone!'

A flock of the rainbow lollies coloured the sky above them, just like Cami's dream. She sighed happily, her worries about the funfair rides evaporating quicker than a puff of steam from a warm jam tart.

'And just look at the view!' Dee said.

'More colours than I've got in my nose!' Louis barked.

The fair sprawled below them like a multicoloured carnival. There were bright tents and game stalls and food trucks and so many rides that they couldn't count them all! The Summertime Big Wheel rotated slowly in the

middle with carriages painted as citrus fruit circles – orange, grapefruit, lemon and lime – and woven with beautiful orange blossom. It was so magical that Cami decided then and there to only let herself think positive thoughts for the rest of the day.

Nana found a clear patch of land just outside the gates and lowered the banana balloon. 'Off you go and have a sunny time!' she said.

'Bye, Nana Banana!' the super cutes cried, and they ran towards the flags at the fairground entrance.

The fairground was guarded by two fans

called Frida and Fred. They were dressed in navy and gold uniforms, with ribbons streaming from their faces like manes.

'You're just in time for the parade,' said Frida, ushering them through.

The super cutes, jiggling with joy, danced into the Sunflower Fair with smiles stretched across their faces. It was wonderful from the air, but even better on the ground, where the music was so it loud it thrummed in their tummies and delicious hot candy smells wrapped around their faces.

'Where shall we go first?' asked Dee. 'D-force? Candyfloss? The Hoola-hoola dance tent?'

'First, we must get the Summer Shower for

good luck,' said Sammy. 'Follow me!'

'Summer Shower!' Cami gasped. 'This day gets better and better!'

Sammy led them to a giant sunflower. It towered higher than a liquorice tree and it dipped its heavy head to greet them.

'Stand underneath!' Sammy instructed.

They crowded together beneath the flower and held hands as it rained sunshine petals on all of them. The petals stuck in their fur and on their spikes like flakes of pure gold.

'Happy summer, everyone!' the super cutes cried, twirling in the pretty downpour.

'What's that over there?' Cami said, spying something from her position above Pip's head.

'It's shining like a sunrise – but it can't be the sunrise, because the sun has already risen.'

'Ah,' Sammy said, lifting his sunglasses. 'That's the glow cake tent.'

'Mmmm, glow cakes!' said the cutes, licking their lips.

'Do you want me to roll ahead and get some before they run out?' said Micky, getting ready to tuck himself into a piggy-roll position.

Sammy chuckled. 'They never run out. So why don't we have fun at the fair and keep the cakes until the end?'

'I think eating cake before going on a fast whizzy ride might be a mistake,' Pip agreed.

At the words *fast whizzy ride*, Cami's

positive thinking took a tumble. But she managed just in time to turn two raindrops into a miniature cocktail umbrella and a straw before they dropped on Pip's head. Pip now looked like a sparkling drink which made Cami laugh so much, she nearly forgot why she'd wobbled in the first place!

'If we leave the cakes till the end, we can eat them slowly and savour them,' said Dee. 'I'm a cake expert, so trust me – that's how you want to eat cake: slowly, with friends.'

'Great idea,' Lucky laughed. 'Cakes with mates is the perfect way to end a perfect day. What do you think, Cami?'

The little cloud's worries vanished

completely. 'Yes, yes, yes!' she cried. 'Let's do everything the right way to make it a PERFECT day!'

CHAPTER FOUR

The Riddle of the Poppets

'What shall we do first?' Dee asked. 'What can you see up there, Cami?'

'There's so much, I don't know where to begin!' Cami said.

'Follow me!' Louis barked. 'Follow me!'

The super cutes followed the labradoodle,
who was now bouncing through the crowds,
yapping with joy.

'Where's he taking us?' Lucky asked.

'I think I know . . .' Sammy said.

They found Louis standing
and panting by a yellow
booth, strung

with pretty pastel bunting. Behind the counter was a giant net full of bouncing balls that chuckled every time they were tossed into the air, and a big sparkly box.

'Oh, Louis, you can't chase these balls,' Lucky said, laughing. 'They're poppets.'

The giant ping-pong balls giggled as they bounced and bumped into each other.

'No harm in watching, is there?' Louis said, his tail drooping.

'Now we're here, we should find out what it's all about,' said Micky in his most efficient voice. He looked at the poster. 'Let's see . . . Aha, the Sunny Lucky Dip! It says here that we need to put our gifts in the box and then put our name on a poppet and pop it in the net with the others.'

'Pick a poppet and pop it?' said Pip.

'Yes, Pip. Pick a poppet and pop it in the net,' Micky said patiently.

'Can a pup go with Pip and pick a poppet and pop it in the net?' Louis said, catching on to the game. The other super cutes started to giggle.

'Yes, a pup can go with Pip and pick a poppet and ... Hold on a minute,' Micky tutted. 'You're joking with me, aren't you!'

'Yes, we are, Micky!' said Cami, giggling. 'Dee, we should give him a medal or something for being a good sport. Can you make one?'

'I certainly can!' Dee whipped out some felt and made Micky a badge saying *Very Patient Pig!* and pinned it to his bow tie.

The cutes placed their gifts in the box. Dee had made a festival tent that folded down into a tiny cube like a magical piece of origami. Lucky had made a lucky-charm necklace. Micky donated two tickets to the Museum of the Magical and Marvellous. Pip gave a golden winner's rosette.

Louis gave a painting of hug whales he'd done on holiday, and Sammy had written a book full of Interesting Facts and wrapped it up.

'I hope my suncatcher goes to someone who needs some rainbow sparkle,' Cami said with a shy smile, putting her little pouch into the box.

The super cutes each took a ping-pong ball from the basket and wrote their names and threw them back in, where they immediately began bouncing with the other poppets.

There was a sudden toot of horns and a big cheer rose from the crowds. Cami rose up to see what the fuss was about.

'It's the Opening Parade!' she said. 'Let's get closer.'

The crowd was already large, but it didn't

matter as most of the Opening Parade took place in the air. First came the acrobatic apples, thrown into the sky by giant trampolines, where they rolled and tumbled about. Then came the lightbulb lemons, who stood on each other's shoulders until they were a hundred

lemons high and flashed on and off to the beat of the music. Roller skates in silk tutus did aerial displays while the broccoli

brigade tossed ribbons that looped and danced in the air and spelled out *Welcome to the Sunflower Fair.* Everyone cheered.

Then it was time for the final act: the Sunflower Salute.

All the performers took to the air and danced the final number, weaving in and out of each other

with ribbons and lights. Way up high, daytime fireworks erupted in neon yellow, green and orange, bursting into huge light balls, and mini fireworks branched off to make petal shapes. Sunflower after sunflower exploded above the Petal Pasture, making the crowd *oooh* and *aaah*. Instead of fizzing out, the sparks formed the shape of a helter-skelter slide, and all the performing cutes slid down, back to the ground.

'That was amazing!' Cami said.

'Brilliant!' said Micky.

'One of the best I've ever seen,' Sammy said, nodding his approval.

'Next year I want to be a performer,' said Pip. 'I want to jump and fly and do all those things.'

'Me too,' said Lucky. 'Let's do lots of practice and see if we can join the parade.'

'Me three!' said Cami.

Just as Pip was about to attempt a triple-flip-back-roly-poly, there was a shocked gasp from the surrounding cutes.

'WATCH OUT! COMING THROUGH!'

The super cutes jumped aside as little tickets tumbled through, their paper faces far too

serious for the funfair. Something was wrong.

'What's going on?' Sammy asked.

'The poppets!' shouted a ticket, which was quickly blown aside by Fred, the fan.

'Someone let them loose and they've bounced away!' Fred said.

'We can't do the Sunny Lucky Dip without the poppets!' Frida panted.

'Oh, no!' Lucky said. 'What happened?'

'No one knows,' said Fred. 'It's a catastrophe!'

'CATastrophe indeed,' Dee said a little huffily. 'I bet you this has nothing to do with cats.'

Cami floated higher up to see where the poppets might have gone – but something else caught her eye.

'You're right, this has nothing to do with cats,' she said. 'It's more of a dog problem.'

'Don't look at me!' Louis said. 'I only *thought* about chasing the balls. I would never, ever hurt the poppets.'

'I didn't mean you, Louis,' Cami said. 'Another dog.'

'Not? You don't mean? It can't be, not

again . . .' Lucky dipped her head sadly.

'I'm afraid so,' Cami sighed. She rained a little sad sprinkle of water. 'I just spied the Glamour Gang and one of them was looking particularly mischievous.'

'Clive the chihuahua,' they all said.

Clive might have been small, but his attitude was bigger than the Summertime Big Wheel. His diva demands and dramatic antics had ruined talent shows and baking competitions and birthday parties. The chihuahua was never happy unless he was winning something or being the centre of attention, and his tantrums were something else.

'We can't let Clive and his gang ruin

everything,' said Micky.

'Let's chase them out of the fair!' Louis said, preparing a growl.

Lucky shook her head. 'No,' she said firmly. 'Clive might be the most spoilt cute in the whole World of Cute and behave VERY badly sometimes, but we know he has goodness inside him.'

Cami rained down some miniature love hearts that landed on her friends' heads with sweet strawberry pops. 'Remember the Friendship Festival?' she said. 'Lucky showed us how being kind to someone can help them become kind in return. We should try to help the Glamour Gang.'

'All right,' Sammy said, adjusting his glasses.

'Summer is the season for growing things, and that should include patience and kindness.'

'And catnip,' said Dee and the super cutes all giggled.

They set off to find Clive and his friends the muffin, the scooter, the snail and the pizza slice – the self-named Glamour Gang. They were by the Fruit Kebab stall, chomping their watermelon chunks and throwing the skewers over their shoulders.

'Be careful! You might hurt someone,' Dee said angrily.

Clive, wearing a shiny gold jumpsuit with a fruit-bowl hat, swung round to look at them. 'Why are you lot here?' he yapped. 'Come to

admire the best outfit of the day?' He did a full

swirl and slapped a passing hotdog in the eye

with a loose bunch of grapes.

'We want to know why you released the

poppets,' Lucky said sternly.

'Poppets? We don't know anything about

poppets, do we?' Clive fluttered his long eyelashes at his friends, who giggled behind their hands.

'Hang on a moment. What's that?' Cami said, looking down.

The muffin was holding a basket behind his back, full of ordinary yellow ping-pong balls. Every single ball had the Glamour Gang's names on them.

'You're going to replace the poppets with these balls so you win all the Summer Gifts!' Cami said angrily, raining down sad-face emoticons.

'So what?' Clive spat, swatting the emoticons out of the way. 'I spent hours – HOURS – getting ready to look fabulous.

I deserve every single one of those gifts.'

'But the Sunflower Fair is about enjoying summer, not fashion, Clive,' Sammy said.

'Who says you can't have both, hmmm? HMMM?' Clive's front legs trembled a little. 'And, anyway, you can't stop me. We've already put four baskets of ping-pong balls in the bouncy net.'

'IS THAT SO!'

Standing at Clive's feet was the owner of the huge, booming, foghorn voice – the small but ferociously forthright Tallulah the ticket master. Clive struck a pose to show off his gold glittery suit, but Tallulah was not to be dazzled. Micky's little piggy cheeks flushed pink to purple with awe. Not that Tallulah noticed. She was

eyeballing Clive with a stare that could freeze all the barbecues in the land.

'If the poppets aren't back in place within the hour,' she boomed, 'you will be banished from the Sunflower Fair FOREVER – you and all your friends.'

Clive held his pose, but his lip began to wobble.

With one final stare at the Glamour Gang, Tallulah disappeared into the crowd. The super cutes looked at Clive. His face was scrunched, his whiskers were quivering, one eyelid was twitching . . . They knew what was coming . . .

'SQUEE-RAAA-RAA-RAAL!'

Clive's high-pitched howl was quickly

followed by a stamping of all four paws and a snarl that revealed his sharp little teeth. Then he squealed again. And again.

Louis covered his ears. 'Stop it! Stop it!'

'NO!' Clive yelled. 'I'm FURIOUS.'

'Well, what do you want *us* to do about it?' Dee said, losing her own temper.

'Be NICE TO ME,' Clive yapped, staring at them all with bulging eyes.

Everything was getting a little too heated, Cami thought. She blew a light vanilla breeze, hoping it would sweeten the mood. Instead it blew a strawberry off the top of Clive's hat, which rolled down his head and bopped him on the nose.

Startled by the fruity interruption, Clive stopped squealing.

'Oops!' Cami spluttered, and started to giggle.

Then they all did. Including Clive. In fact, he enjoyed the attention so much, he spun round three times, did a little curtsey and fluttered his eyelashes. The super cutes couldn't help it – they cheered.

'You love me! You love me!' Clive sang.

'You're still in trouble,' Micky grunted.

'You're not being very patient, Mucky,' Clive tutted, prodding Micky's *Very Patient Pig!* badge.

Micky went red with fury. 'It's not Mucky, it's Micky!'

'And I think we've been patient enough with you, Clive,' Pip added, rolling her eyes acrobatically.

But Clive wasn't listening. He had turned to his Glamour Gang and was asking what they thought of his new pose.

CHAPTER FIVE

Rain on the Parade

Lucky took her friends to one side. 'We have to help the Glamour Gang,' she said.

'But that dog needs to learn a lesson,' Dee hissed. 'We should let Tallulah throw them out. What do you think, Sammy?'

Sammy sighed. 'Never in the history of the Sunflower Fair has there been such a show of selfishness,' he said.

Lucky flapped her wings for attention. 'If one cute in the World of Cute is sad, then we can't say that the World of Cute is happy,' she insisted. 'We all need to work together to put things right.'

Clive ran around trying to listen, barking and yipping. Every time the cutes turned to send him away, he struck little poses and blew little kisses.

'He is a disgrace to dogs,' Louis growled.

Cami saw how sad Clive's behaviour was making Lucky. The happiness of her friends was more important than anything. 'I agree with Lucky,' she said. 'The sooner we help the Glamour Gang, the sooner we can ALL get back to having fun.'

Pip backflipped and landed perfectly, for once. 'I agree!' she said.

'Me too,' said Dee.

'Me three,' said Micky.

'What are friends FOUR!' said Lucky, giving Cami a big wink.

Sammy beckoned over the Glamour Gang as well as the super cutes. 'Here's what we're all going to do,' he said. 'We'll head off in different directions and round up the poppets. We'll close in like a net and get them back to the booth.'

'I can get the ones that bounce high,' Pip said, leaping in the air and landing with a thwump on her side. 'Oops.'

'And I can make some nets to catch them in,' said Dee, already rummaging in her giant craft pockets.

'Scooter, you can zoom round the back of the poppets and send them our way,' Micky instructed. 'Pizza and Muffin, do your best. Because if you don't . . . you'll have Tallulah to talk to. Although I'll happily talk to her for you. I mean, if it's easier.' He blushed again.

'I don't want to be thrown out of the fair,' the pizza sniffed.

Micky clapped his hands, checking to see if Tallulah was watching. Cami thought he was probably trying to impress the ticket master. 'Then let's get to work!' he said.

The Glamour Gang and the super cutes began to round up the poppets. All apart from Clive, who climbed on to Lucky's back.

'You too, Clive,' Sammy said. 'You caused this mess.'

'Can't,' Clive snapped. 'After everything that's happened, I'm exhausted.' He blinked hard and pressed one paw dramatically against his forehead.

Lucky tipped him off her back.

'Come on, Clive! Use your paws. You can still help us by spotting poppets,' Cami said, encouragingly.

'FINE,' Clive grumbled. 'Ooh, there's one. There's one. Another one there!'

With lots of effort and plenty of team work, finally every last poppet was back in the basket in time for the Sunny Lucky Dip event. The poppets juggled and jiggled with excitement as all the cutes gathered round the booth.

Melly the mop was the Summer Gift giver. The cutes drummed their feet as he reached over the net to pluck the first name.

He grabbed a chuckling poppet and read the writing.

'And the name is . . . Terry the tambourine!'

Terry jingle-jangled with happiness as he plucked his gift from the box. A painting!

'That's mine!' Louis yipped.

'Thanks, Louis,' Terry said with a happy rattle. 'I love the hug whales!'

Melly plucked another poppet. 'The next name is . . . Clive the chihuahua!'

'Well done, Clive!' Cami cried, and Lucky turned to give him an encouraging smile.

Clive strutted up to the box and dipped his paw into the pile of gifts. He picked one up and put it back again, then rummaged some more.

'I think he's looking for the biggest,'

Pip whispered. 'Typical Clive.'

Clive eventually settled for a large gift-wrapped box of luxury chocolates. He waved it for everyone to see.

Melly tapped his microphone. 'And next we have . . . Clive the chihuahua? Again?'

'Lots of presents for me,' Clive yipped. Without a whisker of hesitation, he jumped into the gift box. He emerged holding some fruitini-boppers with bouncy kiwi chunks. He couldn't put on the boppers because of his giant hat, so he tucked them in his handbag.

'After all the trouble we went to, you still put your name in twice?' Dee scolded. 'Naughty dog.'

'Oh, Clive,' Pip said. 'I should prickle you this very moment for being so selfish.'

Clive put his paws in his ears and shouted 'LA LA LA!' to drown out their tellings-off. Louis began to growl, Pip to tut, Lucky to flap and Dee to flex her claws. Sammy had fallen asleep.

Cami was still determined to have a wonderful day, so she whispered, 'Don't let him ruin it for the rest of us. Let's enjoy the Summer Gift giving!'

The super cutes agreed that Clive couldn't be allowed to ruin the mood, so they decided to ignore him.

Soon the Petal Pasture was filled with cries of delight as cutes received scarves and decorations and trinkets. Cami didn't see who had picked her rainbow suncatcher, but she hoped it was someone who needed colour in their life!

'And that's it, folks!' said Melly. 'Now everyone must go and enjoy the sunshine.'

'Wait,' Cami said. 'I haven't had my turn yet.'

Melly looked worried. 'But there are no gifts left,' he said, tipping the Sunny Lucky Dip box to show it was empty. 'I must have done it wrong, somehow. What a muddle! It's all my fault.'

'I don't think it was your fault at all,' Sammy

said, looking over at Clive. The chihuahua was scoffing his luxury chocolates and not giving any of them to the rest of the Glamour Gang.

'Of course,' Melly said sadly. 'I'm so sorry, Cami. Clive took an extra present, which means there weren't enough to go round.'

'The gift doesn't really matter,' Cami said, putting on a brave smile. 'I don't need a gift. Having all my friends around me is all I really wanted today, anyway.'

'But everyone needs something to go home with,' Melly said, swishing his mop in despair. 'We can't let you leave empty-handed.'

'I'll take home lots of memories,'

Cami said, puffing up her cloud fluff. 'That's the best gift of all, isn't it?'

'THIS WON'T DO!' yelled Tallulah the ticket master suddenly, shocking all the cutes so they fell over each other like dominos. Micky jumped and straightened his tie.

'We . . . we . . . collected all the poppets,' the scooter piped up. 'Please don't throw us out.'

'NO,' bellowed Tallulah. 'I mean, it will not do that one our wonderful cutes is left without a Summer Gift. So I will give you one myself, Cami.'

'As many goes on the rides as she likes?' Pip suggested.

'An extra glow cake!' Louis said.

'A tour of the Sunshine Cakery?' Dee suggested, licking her whiskers.

'I'm not telling you. It'll be a wonderful surprise,' Tallulah said. She winked at Cami. 'I'll be back later to fetch you.'

'Thank you!' Cami blushed with joy. Her cloud fluff flashed all the colours of the rainbow and rained little popping watermelons. 'Thank you so much!'

'NO PROBLEM!' shouted Tallulah and marched back into the crowds.

'I can't wait to see what your surprise Summer Gift is, Cami!' Lucky said, trotting on the spot.

'Me neither,' said Clive. 'Bagsy I go first, whatever it is.'

'Wait a minute,' said Dee. 'You've caused a total DOGastrophe, and you expect to be invited along to Cami's special tour? I don't think so!'

Clive smoothed back his whiskers. 'It's only right, you know. After all, my ancestors practically built the World of Cute –'

'I don't think that's entirely true,' Sammy said.

'It is. It is, it is, it is,' yapped Clive. 'My relatives, the Pawstons and the Barkalots, were the most respected cutes in all the land.'

'Whatever you say, Clive,' Pip said with a giggle.

'We don't care if you are a Pawston or a Barkalot or even a Little Ratterton!' Dee said. 'In the World of Cute, you don't automatically get everything you want just because of your name. You have to be kind, considerate and *cute*.'

Clive made a high-pitched growl that wobbled his cheeks. He looked at Lucky for her usual kindness. But even Lucky's patience had run out. Her horn began to fizz . . . and an army of clothes pegs burst out of it and nipped at

Clive's dainty little feet. One peg leaped up and gripped his nose.

'Ow! Dell id do dop!' Clive said through his clenched teeth and blocked nostrils.

'Tell it to stop?' said Lucky. 'Sorry, Clive. My luna-horn has a mind of its own and it doesn't like it when my friends are unhappy.'

'And you did rob Cami of her Sunny Lucky Dip gift,' Pip added.

Clive quivered with rage. Then he stuck his paw in his handbag, where he rummaged theatrically before bringing out the kiwi fruitini-boppers. He presented them to Cami.

'Didn't like dem eddyway,' he grumbled.

The clothes pegs disappeared with a POP.

Clive inhaled deeply through his little unpegged nostrils.

'Thank you, Clive, it's lovely,' Cami said, ignoring his comment and popping the headband on top of her head.

The kiwis bounced and bopped as Cami twirled for everyone to see, causing a mini tornado. Nobody minded, especially as she showered down little popping miniature deckchairs, which was random but very cute. Even Clive couldn't help but wag his little tail. Cami, now looking dazzling with her sunshine ribbon and kiwi fruitini-boppers, expanded with happiness like an inflatable white marshmallow.

'Queen of the Sunflower Fair!' said Sammy.

'Yes, Queen of the Sunflower Fair!' everyone agreed – apart from Clive, of course, who considered himself the only royal in the World of Cute!

CHAPTER SIX

That's the Spirit!

With everyone happy again, the super cutes rushed off to explore the fair. There was jewellery-making and kite-flying and flag-pole racing. Pip won a prize for getting her kite the highest. Sammy won the World of Cute Trivia Quiz by a mile – quite literally, when he worked out that one mile was the length of three hundred pillow snakes. Dee won a prize at the crafting station for making the longest flower chain with felt sunflowers. And all of them jumped for joy on Cushion Mountain.

When they finally got off the giant springy beanbag, giggling and exhausted, they looked around to see what was next.

'I think it's time,' Micky said.

'Time for what, Micky?' Cami asked.

'Time for a ride!' Pip squealed. 'That one first! That one first!'

She was pointing to a golden rollercoaster which was flying in and around candyfloss clouds.

'Ah, yes, The Zim-Zoomer is the most popular ride at the Sunflower Festival,' said

Sammy with a yawn. 'You go ahead, Pip. I may take the opportunity to have a little snooze.'

'You snooze, you lose!' Pip said, bouncing off to the ride.

As she watched the Zim-Zoomer cars whizzing round the rollercoaster loops, Cami couldn't help feeling a little relieved that it wasn't a group activity. Cami and all the super cutes on the ground watched Pip as she zipped up and down and round and round, gleefully licking the sweet cloud puffs as she passed, and yelling to go even faster. When the ride ended, she wobbled towards the super cutes like a pineapple jelly.

'That was amazing,' she said, her dizzy

feet taking her off to one side, then back again. 'Let's all go on one together next. It would be maximum super cute excitement!'

'Perhaps it's time for the new ride the dipsy daisies told me about,' said Micky. 'They said it was just beyond the Parasol Pond. Over there!'

On the opposite side of the field was a barn, where a giant sign said:

'Very odd,' Sammy said, scratching his bottom, which usually helped him think better. 'A Rain Ride at a summer fair?'

'Could be refreshing,' said Louis. 'I get a bit hot under my fur coat.'

As they walked towards the new ride, a light breeze picked up. It flipped the bunting, making the whole fair flutter. It also blew away a large bunch of balloons that had been floating in front of the sign. The full name of the mysterious ride became clear.

THE ROLLERGHOSTER GHOST TRAIN

'A Ghost Train!' Louis barked. 'Barking at ghosts is going to be so much fun!'

'I can't wait!' Dee said. 'I love getting thrills!'

'And I love getting chills!' Pip said, launching into a cartwheel. 'Cami, do you want to sit next to me?'

'Um . . .' Cami shrank back. As hard as she tried to keep her positive attitude, it appeared to have run away completely.

'What's the matter?' Lucky said. 'You're turning grey. Don't you want to go?'

Cami saw how happy and excited her friends were to go on the new ride. Spending the day with them was so special. With everything finally working out again after the chaos of

Clive, she couldn't let her nerves get in the way of a good time.

'I'm fine,' she said brightly, forcing her cloud fluff to puff up. 'Absolutely fine. Let's go!'

The announcer's voice boomed scarily from inside the barn. It made the cutes tingle with excitement.

'Welcome to the spookiest rollercoaster ride in the World of Cute.

'If you dare . . . prepare for a scare!'

Cami let out a little squeak. Then a shriek. And try as she might to stop it, her cloud fluff got moodier and refused to stay fluffy and white. She wasn't sure she WAS prepared to be

scared, after all! What was she

going to do?

She dropped

some rain. This

time it wasn't

a cute shower

of little rabbits

or mini lightbulbs.

It was wet, cold water.

Her friends looked up at her with concern.
Cami had shrunk to half her size, and was
purple and blue like a bruise.

'It's okay to be nervous,' Sammy said.
'We all feel nervous about different things!'

'We don't all have to go on the Ghost Train,' Lucky said in support.

'I was too nervous to go on the Zim-Zoomer with Pip,' Micky said.

'Me too!' said Dee.

'Well, you're a scaredy-cat, Dee. I'm not scared of Ghost Trains,' Clive said, trotting over. 'I'm not scared of anything, EVER. I come from a long line of adventurous hounds, such as –'

'Ahem.' Sammy gave Clive a very stern eye. 'I seem to recall you were scared of being away from home when we went to the Adventure School.'

Clive opened his mouth to speak, but Pip got there before him.

'And you're always scared of people not

thinking you're fashionable, which is a silly thing to be scared of,' she said.

Clive's jowls trembled with annoyance. He usually liked it when people were talking about him, but only when they said things he wanted to hear!

'Look, there's Lady Wah Wah!' he said, to divert attention.

Everyone turned to see the famous microphone pop-star, who wasn't really there.

'You just missed her,' Clive said, tutting.

Lucky smiled at Cami. 'If you don't want to go on the Rollerghoster, then don't. We love you just the way you are.'

Cami looked at her amazing friends and

realised that sometimes being truthful was the brave thing to do. 'I am a bit scared and I don't want to go on the Rollerghoster,' she said boldly, feeling herself fluff up with relief. She giggled. 'In fact, I think it sounds like the ghastliest ghostliest ride ever invented!'

Lucky laughed. Pip squeaked. Micky chuckled. Clive snickered and Sammy guffawed.

'WE NEED HELP!'

The cutes jumped back in alarm as Tallulah strode between them.

'ANYONE FREE TO HELP AT THE GLOW CAKE STAND?' demanded the Ticket Master. 'WHAT ABOUT YOU, CAMI?'

Cami looked at her friends. 'If I go, we

won't be together and today was all about being together,' she said a little sadly.

'But we will be together again in a little while,' said Lucky. 'Go on. It's an honour to hand out glow cakes. It will be something to remember forever.'

'And we'll meet you at the glow cake stall right after the ride,' said Pip.

Cami hesitated. 'Are you sure?' she said.

Pip leaped up and spiked Cami's cloud fluff. 'Yes!' she said. 'Now go before that fierce little ticket chooses someone else for the job.'

Cami waved goodbye to her friends before floating off to the glow cake stall. A large queue was already forming. She was so happy to be able to help out!

She took her position behind the counter and handed out the glorious glowing sunshine goodies one by one, watching the faces of the cutes light up like buttercups as they raised the bright icing to their lips. Her friends were right. This was a special job. And Sammy was right when he said they never ran out! And the cutes

kept on coming. Cami got to say hello to them all. Bella Bubble Tea and Bembe Book, Charlie Cheeseplant and Ethan the egg timer, Petra the pelican and her little pelicaninis . . .

After a while, Cami realised that she hadn't seen her friends yet. They were supposed to come to the glow cake stall right after their ride. Ghost Train rides couldn't take that long, surely?

CHAPTER SEVEN

Toots and Woos

Kitty Kite took over the glow cake stall while Cami went to find her friends.

'Have you seen the super cutes?' she asked everyone she met.

But the answer was always no. That meant one thing. They were still on the ride! Something was wrong. And Cami had to go into the Rollerghoster to find out what was happening.

Gulping back a downpour of fear, Cami approached the Rollerghoster. It had stopped being booming and scary. Instead, it was muttering to itself and occasionally making short sharp shrieks. Cami approached the ride master's cabin.

Liberty the lilo was in charge. She was deflating in despair, then re-inflating and shouting in panic before deflating again.

'What's the matter?' Cami said.

Liberty reinflated and spoke into her voice-changing microphone.

'The best Ghost Train in the world is stuck. If you dare to go in, you'll need plenty of luck.'

'How do we unstick it?' Cami asked.

Liberty let all her air out and slid under the table. 'I've tried everything,' she said with a final puff of despair. 'The train driver's given up and I can't get her to move!'

Cami took a deep breath. I need to pull myself together, she told herself. I have to shake off my fear and do what needs to be done.

The little cloud spun round and round in circles, creating a mini twister. The faster Cami spun, the windier it got. The summer flags flapped and the bunting flipped and the nearby cutes all cheered. 'Go Cami!' they shouted. 'Go on!'

'Cami! Cami! Cami!' everyone else joined in.

The cheers filled Cami with confidence.

She felt her cloud fluff expand and her heart fill with determination. Faster and faster she went until she felt full to the brim with bravery.

'Yes, go Cami,' she whispered to herself.

And she pushed through the giant barn doors of the Rollerghoster Ride.

It was dark inside. Neon ghosts flashed and swooped like bright tissues from one side to the other, wailing **'WOOOOOOOO!'** But they didn't sound particularly scary. Cami stopped and listened harder.

'We don't know what to doooooooo . . .'

Ah! Now that the train was stuck, the ghosts were in a flap.

'Don't worry, ghosties,' Cami said. 'Leave it to me.'

Cami ventured further into the darkness. The train was stuck halfway up the loop of the

rollercoaster. Samaya the sushi-roll was sitting
at the controls, looking cross.

'Too many passengers!' she huffed.
'I cannot go forward with this many passengers!'

'Cami, is that you?' called Pip. 'Help!'

Cami floated closer to the carriage and
covered her friends in comforting cloud fluff.

'It's okay, I'm going to help you,' she said. 'Where's Sammy?'

Sammy had fallen asleep and his fur had camouflaged to fit the surrounding darkness. At the sound of his name, he woke up and turned bright green.

'We're stuck!' he exclaimed.

'Yes,' Cami said. 'Apparently there are too many of you in the carriage.'

'And we all know why,' Micky tutted. 'One of the Glamour Gang snuck on at the last minute.'

Cami drifted closer. The muffin was sitting next to Clive, and both of them were looking shaken. The muffin had sunk down into his muffin case and the fruit on Clive's hat was trembling.

'He wouldn't wait for the next ride,' Lucky sighed.

'Because if I waited for the next ride, I wouldn't get to sit with my friend, Clive!' the muffin wailed.

'And if you hadn't screamed so loudly when the pink ghost arrived, the train driver would never have known,' Clive huffed, turning his back on the naughty cake. 'As soon as she saw you, it stopped.'

'I just wanted to sit with you!' The muffin sounded hurt.

'I understand. Sometimes you'll do anything to be with your friends,' Cami said. 'I'm sure Samaya understands that.'

'I do NOT!' Samaya grumped. 'It's against the rules. Rules are rules.'

'Everyone knows I LOVE rules,' Micky said. 'But Samaya, if we don't keep going, we'll be stuck up here for the rest of the fair.'

Samaya crossed her arms. She wasn't going anywhere.

'Get me out! Get me off this train!' Clive yipped.

'Calm down, panicky pup,' Dee said.

'Or I'll make you a muzzle.'

'What are we going to do?' Pip asked, peering over the edge of the rails. 'If I jump from here . . . I'll be a smoothie!'

The train was too high up for any of the cutes to get out. Making Samaya the sushi-roll move the train was the only way. With all the passengers jittery and scared, Cami knew it was up to her.

She floated in front of the train. 'I think the cutes have learned their lesson now. Why don't you finish the loop and take them back down?'

Samaya blasted her horn. **TOOOOOOOOOOT!** It sounded angry, but Cami noticed Samaya's eyes were wet with tears. She wasn't cross. She was scared.

'You're nervous, but there's no need to be,' Cami said softly, dabbing at Samaya's tears with her fluff.

'I-I've only ever driven with the right number of passengers on board,' sniffed Samaya. 'I'm not sure I can do it!'

'I think you can,' Cami said. 'You know, I was too scared to even come near the Rollerghoster and now look at me. I knew I had to help my friends. Tell yourself that you're saving the day – and drive.'

'It's th-th-that easy?' Samaya stuttered.

Cami made her fluff as lovely and soft as can be and blew a wasabi-flavoured breeze to help fill the sushi-roll with fiery determination. 'Come on, Samaya,' she said temptingly. 'Chase me! Catch the treats!'

Cami edged away, raining soy-sauce fish bottles. Samaya moved the train forward bit by bit. The dark tunnel was full of the sound of happy squeals and all the fear disappeared.

'We're moving!' the cutes cheered. 'Go, Samaya!'

Samaya managed a shy smile. The train picked up speed. She followed Cami up, round and down the track, all the way back to the embarking platform at the bottom.

'I did it!' she exclaimed.

'You did and you did it brilliantly,' Cami said,

bopping her on the head with her fluff.

TOOOOOOOOOOOOOOOT!

went the Rollerghoster horn.

The cutes clapped Samaya the sushi-roll as they jumped off the train one by one. 'Well done, well done, Samaya!'

'Well done to Cami,' Samaya said. 'I couldn't have done it without her.'

'Ahem.' The muffin stepped forward. 'I just want to say sorry for causing so many problems.'

'Well,' said Samaya. 'That is a happy ending. And if you'd all like to have another ride, then be my guest!'

'I think I'll sit this one out,' said the muffin.

'Me too,' said Clive, who was trembling

like a leaf.

'That means there's a spare space, Cami,' said Sammy, waggling his glasses. 'You want a go?'

TOOOOOOOT!

'You bet!' Cami said. 'Especially as my friend is driving.'

CHAPTER EIGHT

What Goes Around . . .

After the Rollerghoster, the Super cutes strolled back into the main field.

'It must be time for our glow cakes now,' Dee said, eyes twinkling.

'Well, we've certainly earned them,' Sammy chuckled.

'NOT YET!' Tallulah the ticket master shouted. She screeched to a halt and tapped each of the super cutes on the foot. 'First, it's Cami's surprise.'

'I thought helping on the glow cakes stall was my present!' Cami gasped.

'No, that was a job,' said Tallulah. 'Your present is right now. All of you, follow me!'

The cutes looked at each other and shrugged. What could it be?

They followed Tallulah round the Catch-a-Candy stall, through the dipsy daisy dance display, across the pelican croquet pitch and to a gate at the very furthest end of the Petal Pasture.

The ticket master looked at the super cutes in turn.

'Stay quiet and walk carefully,' she ordered. Then she opened the gates slowly . . .

The super cutes gasped!

Then they squealed!

Then they made 'aw!' noises and sighed happily.

There, right in front of them, was a field of baby sunflowers, swaying in the sunshine. Grown-up sunflowers stooped over them, stroking them with their large soft leaves.

'A sunflower nursery!' Cami said, hovering above a gaggle of little ones. 'Can I give them a present?'

'Of course!' Tallulah said.

Cami rained down a gentle mist of sunshine

droplets. The baby flowers shook their heads and laughed.

'I can't believe it,' said Louis, who had begun to sketch the scene with his magical nose. 'It's going to be a masterpiece. I'll call it *Sunflowers*.'

'Well, what else would you call it!' Pip said with a giggle.

'If I'm not mistaken, flowerlings love to sing,' Sammy said. 'Shall we try?'

'Yes! Let's see if they'll copy our song,' Lucky said.

We're all off to the Sunflower Fair
Wearing yellow in our fur, fluff and hair.

It's super funtime all day long

Everybody join in our Sunflower Song!

One by one the sunflowers joined in until the prettiest, sunniest chorus rippled across the field. Then the babies began to yawn. They lifted their faces to the sun and gulped at the air before closing their eyes and swaying side to side. The large sunflowers began shushing them, soft and humming like the sound of a gentle breeze, and the baby flowerlings fell asleep one by one.

Tallulah gently ushered the super cutes out of the field, back towards the fair.

'How was that?' she asked Cami.

'I feel so lucky,' Cami sighed. 'I've had the BEST day at the Sunflower Fair. Everything has turned out brilliantly. It always does when I'm with my friends.'

'That's because friendship makes everything better,' Lucky said.

'And you showed the very best kind of friendship,' Micky said. 'To put your fears aside to help your friends – that's special, you know.'

'You're a real ray of sunshine, Cami,' Pip said, backflipping and landing perfectly.

'Oh my goodness!' Sammy said suddenly. 'Look over there!'

Just ahead of them was a glittering carousel, with bluebird-shaped seats and golden poles.

A sweet music filled the air.

'Where did that come from?' Cami gasped. 'It wasn't there before.'

'Well I never!' said Sammy in amazement. 'It's the Kindness Carousel!'

'The what?' Louis barked.

'The Kindness Carousel . . .' Sammy looked dreamy. 'It's a rare and wonderful thing. It's attracted to acts of friendship and understanding, and the last time it was seen was in the year –'

'Tell us later, Sammy! What are we waiting for!' Pip squealed and tumbled like an out-of-control acrobat towards the carousel, with Micky piggy-rolling beside her.

'Come on Sammy, come on Dee!' Lucky said, flapping with excitement. 'It's starting to turn!'

Cami watched as her friends ran on to the spinning ride, grabbed the golden columns and swung themselves on to the bluebird seats. She was so thrilled that she couldn't move. She would have been happy to just float for the rest

of the day, watching the sparkle of the fair and the joy of her friends. But their voices broke through her happy haze.

'Cami!' they called. 'Cami, come on!'

Sammy, Dee, Micky, Louis, Pip and Lucky took turns to call and wave as their seats passed by. And there was one bluebird left. Cami took

her place among her friends. The Kindness Carousel went faster and faster, whirling shafts of golden light like a giant twirling sunflower, and the cutes sang songs and cheered and it felt like summer would last forever.

When the carousel finally slowed down, the Super cutes jumped off and waved goodbye as the incredible machine dissolved into thin air.

'That was the most beautiful thing I've ever seen,' Cami said. 'I don't think any day could have been more perfect.'

'It's not over yet,' said a little yippy voice.

Clive gave a piercing whistle that made Louis' ears stand on end. The scooter appeared, carrying a glowing basket.

'Glow cakes!' Dee said. Unable to hide her excitement, she let out a purr as loud as a brown bear's growl, and everyone laughed.

'I thought we could have them now to finish off our day.' Clive blinked at everyone, waiting for a reaction.

'That's a lovely idea, Clive,' Lucky said. 'You really are a good friend when you want to be.'

The super cutes and the Glamour Gang sat down in a big circle where the carousel had been. They took turns talking about parts of the day they thought were fun, funny or special. And then, on the count of three, they munched their glow cakes all at the same time, grinning as the sublime fizzy-pop flavour tingled their tongues, and sighing as the delicious cream centres filled their tums.

They stayed and played until the sun set and the moon flew up to take its place. As soon as it did, Lucky the lunacorn's horn lit up like

a blue beacon. As the cutes cheered Lucky's special moon-time talent, her horn erupted in a shower of fairy lights that hung in the air like little white suns.

But in the distance, Cami spotted other

colours – a twinkling of red, green and purple – getting closer and closer.

And then Cami saw Albi, the allsort bug who wouldn't come out of his dark hole in the liquorice tree, twirling the suncatcher in his hands. So he *had* come to the Sunflower Fair! And even better, he'd won her Summer Gift!

'Is that your suncatcher?' Dee said, watching the bug trundle past.

'Uh-huh!' Cami gulped and nodded, so happy she could hardly speak. 'I can't believe he was brave enough to come along!'

'I bet he's glad he did,' Pip said. 'Because he's going home with a beautiful gift. It's SOOOOOO pretty. How did you make it?'

'Well, to make a rainbow you just need a little rain and a little sun,' Cami said.

'A bit like something else I can think of,' Lucky said, winking.

'I don't understand,' said Cami.

'I believe Lucky means that a mixture of sunny and rainy *feelings* can also make a sort of rainbow,' said Sammy. 'A special rainbow that makes everyone individual. Good and bad, all mixed up together.'

Cami realised what her friends were saying. That everyone had their fears as well as their excitements. It made them who they were, and it was nothing to be ashamed of. Just like how a little rain and a little sun make a rainbow.

At the sound of squawking, Cami looked up at the sky. A flock of popsicle parrots were flying overhead. Even in the moonlight, they were all bright and beautiful, shiny and sleek, flapping in formation. Apart from one, who was flying upside down and singing out of tune. Cami didn't know why, but it was the funniest, sweetest thing she'd ever seen.

Then she understood.

'I get it!' she said. 'We're all different, but still PERFECTLY CUTE!'

COMING SOON!

Check out more ADVENTURES with the Super Cutes!

Enjoyed Super Cute? Check out these other brilliant books by Pip Bird!

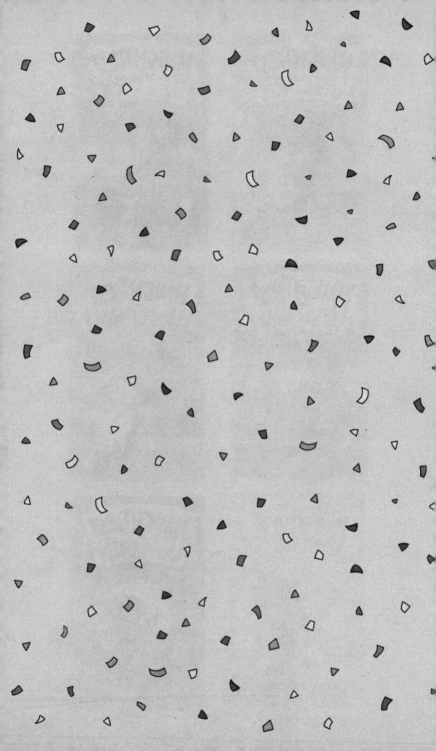